Dear Parents:

Congratulations! Your child is taking the first steps on an exciting journey. The destination? Independent reading!

STEP INTO READING® will help your child get there. The program offers five steps to reading success. Each step includes fun stories and colorful art or photographs. In addition to original fiction and books with favorite characters, there are Step into Reading Non-Fiction Readers, Phonics Readers and Boxed Sets, Sticker Readers, and Comic Readers—a complete literacy program with something to interest every child.

Learning to Read, Step by Step!

Ready to Read **Preschool–Kindergarten**
• big type and easy words • rhyme and rhythm • picture clues
For children who know the alphabet and are eager to begin reading.

Reading with Help **Preschool–Grade 1**
• basic vocabulary • short sentences • simple stories
For children who recognize familiar words and sound out new words with help.

Reading on Your Own **Grades 1–3**
• engaging characters • easy-to-follow plots • popular topics
For children who are ready to read on their own.

Reading Paragraphs **Grades 2–3**
• challenging vocabulary • short paragraphs • exciting stories
For newly independent readers who read simple sentences with confidence.

Ready for Chapters **Grades 2–4**
• chapters • longer paragraphs • full-color art
For children who want to take the plunge into chapter books but still like colorful pictures.

STEP INTO READING® is designed to give every child a successful reading experience. The grade levels are only guides; children will progress through the steps at their own speed, developing confidence in their reading. The F&P Text Level on the back cover serves as another tool to help you choose the right book for your child.

Remember, a lifetime love of reading starts with a single step!

For Mom and Dad
—F.G.

To Emily and Amelia
—E.U.

Visit us on the Web!
StepIntoReading.com
rhcbooks.com

Educators and librarians, for a variety of teaching tools, visit us at RHTeachersLibrarians.com

Library of Congress Cataloging-in-Publication Data
Names: Gilbert, Frances, author. | Unten, Eren Blanquet, illustrator.
Title: I love my tutu! / by Frances Gilbert ; illustrated by Eren Unten.
Description: New York : Random House, [2019]
Summary: A young girl learns that there is a time and a place for everything, including wearing her beloved tutu.
Identifiers: LCCN 2018036826 | ISBN 978-0-525-64753-9 (trade) | ISBN 978-0-525-64754-6 (lib. bdg.) | ISBN 978-0-525-64755-3 (ebook)
Subjects: | CYAC: Tutus (Ballet skirts)—Fiction. | Clothing and dress—Fiction.
Classification: LCC PZ7.1.G547 Iaj 2019 | DDC [E]—dc23

Printed in the United States of America
10 9 8 7 6 5 4 3 2 1

This book has been officially leveled by using the F&P Text Level Gradient™ Leveling System.

STEP 1 READY TO READ

STEP INTO READING®

I Love My Tutu!

by Frances Gilbert
illustrated by Eren Unten

Random House New York

It is time
to get ready
for school.
I put on my dress.

I put on my socks.

I put on my shoes.

I put on my tutu!

"No, you can not
wear a tutu
to school."

"But I love my tutu!"

It is time to get ready
for swimming lessons.
I put on my swimsuit.
I put on my swim cap.
I put on my swim goggles.

I put on my tutu!

"No, you can not
wear a tutu
for swimming lessons."

"But I love my tutu!"

It is time to get ready for soccer.
I put on my uniform.

I put on my shin guards.

I put on my cleats.

I put on my tutu!

“No, you can not
wear a tutu
for soccer.”

“But I love my tutu!”

"Can I wear my tutu to art class?"

"No, you can not
wear a tutu
to art class."

“Can I wear my tutu camping?”

“No, you can not wear a tutu camping!”

"Can I wear my tutu
to the fair?"

Roller Coaster

"No, you can not wear a tutu to the fair."

“BUT I LOVE MY TUTU!”

“Can I wear my tutu to ballet class?”

"Yes! You can
wear your tutu
to ballet class!"

“I LOVE MY TUTU!”

"We love our tutus, too!"